D1722861

Wild About Wheels

ATVs

by Nancy Dickmann

PEBBLE
a capstone imprint

Pebble Emerge is published by Pebble, an imprint of Capstone.
1710 Roe Crest Drive
North Mankato, Minnesota 56003
www.capstonepub.com

Copyright © 2021 by Capstone. All rights reserved. No part of this publication may be reproduced in whole or in part, or stored in a retrieval system, or transmitted in any form or by any means, electronic, mechanical, photocopying, recording, or otherwise, without written permission of the publisher.

Library of Congress Cataloging-in-Publication Data is available on the Library of Congress website.
ISBN: 978-1-9771-2482-1 (hardcover)
ISBN: 978-1-9771-2524-8 (eBook PDF)

Summary: describes ATVs, including what people use them for, their main parts, and how they work.

Image Credits
Alamy: imageBROKER, 13; Capstone Studio: Karon Dubke, 21; Getty Images: Big Cheese Photo, 12; iStockphoto: chameleonseye, 7, JMichl, 4; Shutterstock: Chaikom, background (tire tracks), Denis Volkov, 10, george photo cm, 19, Inna Levchenko, 14–15, Maciej Kopaniecki, cover, back cover, 17, Media_works, 9, Mike Pellinni, 11, Nomad_Soul, 6, trek6500, 5

Editorial Credits
Editor: Carrie Sheely; Designer: Cynthia Della-Rovere; Media Researcher: Eric Gohl; Production Specialist: Katy LaVigne

All internet sites appearing in back matter were available and accurate when this book was sent to press.

Printed and bound in the USA.
003422

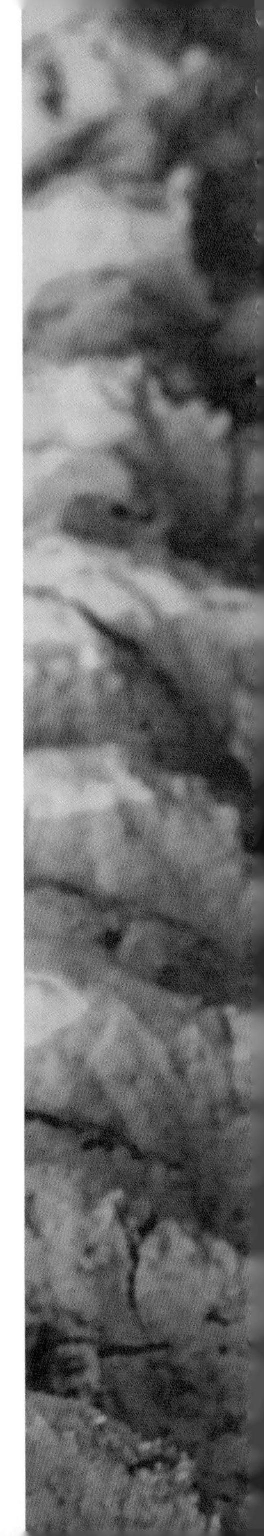

Table of Contents

Words in **bold** are in the glossary.

What ATVs Do

Vroom! An ATV rider zips along a trail. The ATV speeds up and down hills. Dirt flies behind the small **vehicle**.

ATV is short for "all-**terrain** vehicle." These strong machines can go over all types of land. They race across sand. They speed through mud and over bumps.

Why do people ride ATVs? For many, it's just for fun! People like riding ATVs away from regular roads. People ride them into forests. Some people race ATVs on tracks.

But ATVs aren't just for fun. People use ATVs for work. Farmers use ATVs to check on animals and fields. Workers in parks and forests use ATVs too.

Look Inside

Most ATVs have **engines** that run on **gasoline**. These engines provide a lot of power. Some ATVs reach top speeds of 80 miles (129 kilometers) per hour.

Some ATVs run on **electricity**. A **battery** powers them. When the battery is low, it can plug in to charge. Then the ATV can go again!

engine

Trails can be bumpy. But that won't stop ATVs. ATVs have strong shocks. Shocks have springs on the outside. The ATV hits a bump. The spring squeezes. It bounces back. This makes the ride feel less bumpy.

SHIFT

Look Outside

ATVs come in different sizes. Some have two seats to carry two people. Some have a flat space at the back. It is for carrying **cargo**. Some big ATVs can pull trailers.

Most ATVs have four wheels. The tires are wide and bumpy. The bumps help the tires grip the ground. The tires are made of strong rubber.

ATVs have handlebars. The rider steers with them. Most ATVs have a thumb lever by the right handle. It controls the ATV's speed. The harder the rider presses it, the faster the ATV goes.

ATVs have brakes at the front and back. Brakes slow down the ATV. A lever on the right handle controls the front brakes. A foot pedal often controls the back brakes.

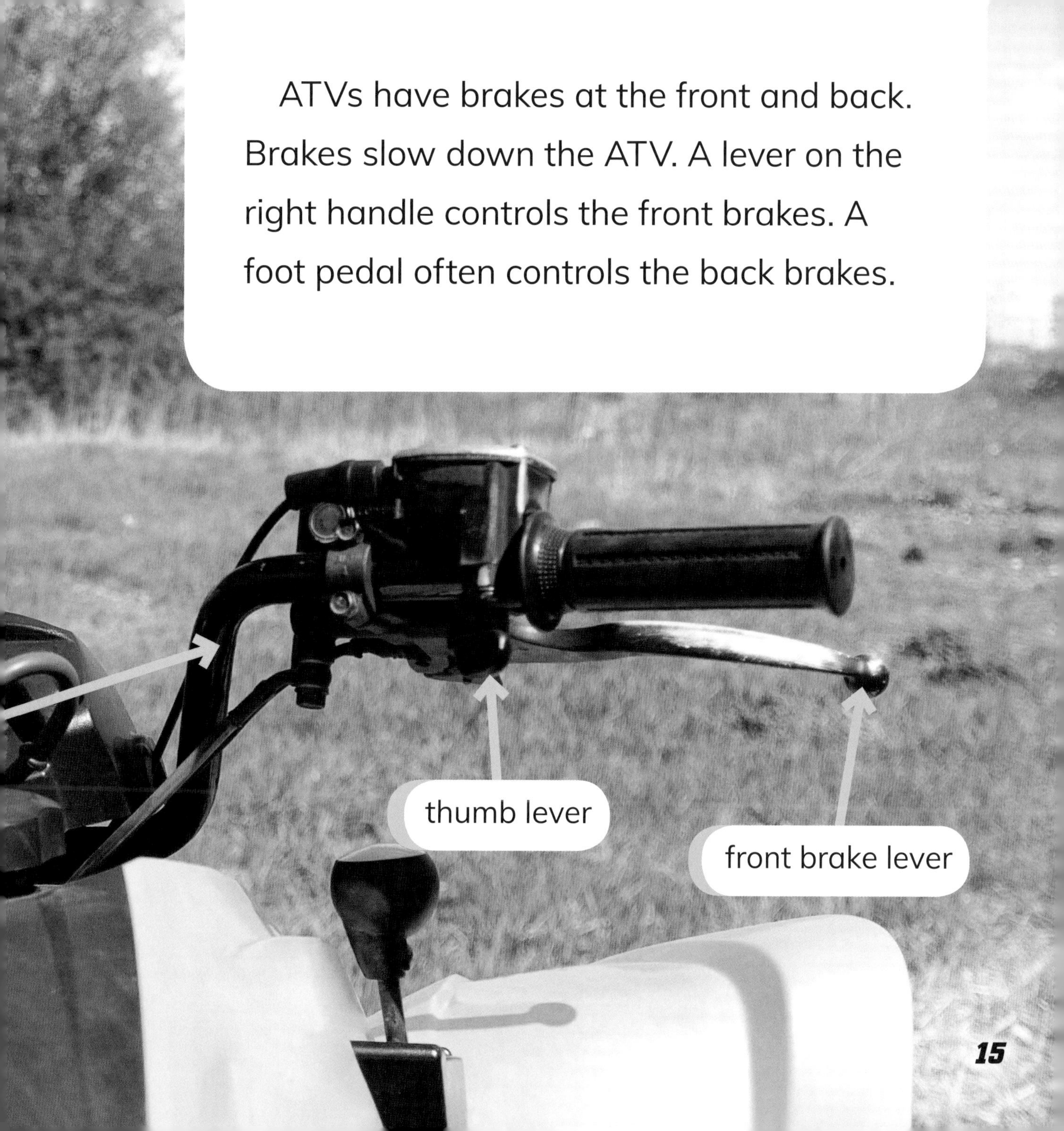

An ATV speeds through the mud. Whoosh! The mud sprays up. It hits the fenders above the ATV's wheels. They keep the rider from getting dirty.

The fenders are lightweight. The less the ATV weighs, the faster it can go. Zoom!

fenders

ATV Diagram

handlebars
seat
cargo area
fenders
tires

Design an ATV

ATVs can go almost anywhere. Choose a place where an ATV can go. Draw an ATV rider going through the place. What will the ATV look like? Is it big or small? Is it carrying cargo? Make sure to give your rider a helmet. Helmets keep riders safe.

Glossary

battery (BA-tuh-ree)—a container that can store and create electricity

cargo (KAHR-goh)—goods being carried

electricity (i-lek-TRI-suh-tee)—electric power that flows along a path; electricity can be used to make machines work

engine (EN-juhn)—a machine in which fuel burns to provide power

gasoline (GA-suh-leen)—a liquid that is often burned in vehicle engines

terrain (tuh-RAYN)—ground or land

vehicle (VEE-uh-kuhl)—a machine that carries people or things

Read More

Abdo, Kenny. *ATVs*. Minneapolis: Abdo Zoom, 2018.

Marx, Mandy R. *ATVs*. North Mankato, MN: Capstone, 2019.

Potts, Nikki. *My First Guide to Fast Vehicles*. Mankato, MN: Capstone, 2017.

Internet Sites

ATV Motocross National Championship
https://atvmotocross.com/

ATV Safety Institute: What is an ATV?
https://atvsafety.org/what-is-an-atv/

Index